Rocky

Rebecca Lisle

Illustrated by Tim Archbold

www.kidsatrandomhouse.co.uk

For Louisa Meadows, ever hopeful...

ROCKY
A CORGI PUPS BOOK 0552 548758

Published in Great Britain by Corgi Books,
an imprint of Random House Children's Books

This edition published 2003

1 3 5 7 9 10 8 6 4 2

Corgi Pups Books are published by Random House Children's Books,
61-63 Uxbridge Road, London W5 5SA,
a division of The Random House Group Ltd,
in Australia by Random house Australia (Pty) Ltd,
20 Alfred Street, Milsons Point, Sydney, NSW 2061, Australia,
in New Zealand by Random House New Zealand Ltd,
18 Poland Road, Glenfield, Auckland 10, New Zealand,
and in South Africa by Random House (Pty) Ltd,
Endulini, 5A Jubilee Road, Parktown 2193, South Africa

THE RANDOM HOUSE GROUP Limited Reg. No. 954009

www.kidsatrandomhouse.co.uk
A CIP catalogue record for this book is available from the British Library.

Printed and bound in Great Britain by
Cox & Wyman Ltd, Reading, Berkshire

Contents

Series Reading Consultant: Prue Goodwin
National Centre for Language and Literacy,
University of Reading

Chapter One

It was *not* Ruby's birthday. It was Jane's birthday.

"Happy Birthday, Jane! Eight today!" Mum and Dad clapped and cheered.

"Huh," said Ruby quietly.

There were seven birthday presents on the kitchen table. There were big parcels and tiny parcels and each was wrapped in different paper.

"You always have more birthdays than me," said Ruby.

"No she doesn't," Mum laughed. "It just feels that way."

"And more presents," whispered Ruby.

"They're lovely," said Jane, smiling. "Thank you!"

And Jane hadn't even opened them. This was just the sort of talk that drove Ruby wild. How did Jane know she'd like them? Ruby was always disappointed with *her* presents. They were never quite what she wanted ... How could Jane be so different?

Slowly, slowly, Jane opened all the presents. It took ages.

"That was only seven presents, and she's eight years old," said Ruby, who had been counting.

Mum brought the eighth present in from the other room. A big red box without a lid. It was making a mewing sound.

"It's just what I've always wanted," said Jane, smiling

happily.

"But you haven't looked yet!" roared Ruby,

jumping up and down.

A beautiful black and white kitten with long, long whiskers poked her head over the edge of the box. "Miaow!"

"Wow! Brilliant, Mum!" Jane grinned.

Ruby didn't think it was brilliant. She wasn't grinning. "It's not fair," she said. "I want one."

"When you're eight you can have your own pet too," said Dad.

"You're not old enough to care for an animal just yet, dear," said Mum.

"Huh," said Ruby. "I bet I could."

The kitten was very sweet. Jane took her into the playroom. Ruby followed.

Jane dangled a strand of wool
in front of the kitten's nose and
the kitten leaped and jumped
and somersaulted trying to
catch it. When Jane
rolled a soft
ball across the
room, the
kitten chased
it and rolled
on it like a
circus cat.

"I want to do that," said Ruby in a small voice.

Jane didn't seem to hear. She snuggled the kitten under her nose and breathed in her smell. "Mmm, Kitty, Kitty, Kitty," she crooned.

"Huh," said Ruby, watching them. "Can I play with her?"

"Sorry, Ruby, but she's mine. I've only just got her."

Jane played with Kitty all day and she would hardly even let Ruby stroke her. "In a few days," she said grandly, "when Kitty's used to us all, then you can play with her, just a bit."

At school the next day, Ruby wrote a long story about her pet puppy.

"I didn't know you had a puppy, Ruby," said Miss Allbright. "What's it called?"

"Piddlypooh," said Ruby quickly. "And I'm afraid Jane isn't allowed to touch him. She's allergic to dogs."

But there wasn't really a pet puppy. It seemed as if there wasn't going to be a pet for her until she was eight years old and that was a long, long way off.

Chapter Two

Down at the bottom of the
garden, in the gloomy place
beneath the lime tree, beside the
compost heap and broken plant
pots, was an old bench. It was
a good place to sit and be sad. So
that's where Ruby went after
school that day.

"It's not fair," she told the rotting tea bags and potato peelings on the compost heap. "I want a pet so badly. Much more than Jane."

She filled her pockets with pebbles and tossed them at the pots. Plink! Plink! Plink!

"I need a pet! I *deserve* a pet!"

Plink! Plink! *Plonk!* Her pebble had bounced against a rock and made an odd sad "plonk" sound. Ruby looked at the rock she'd hit. It had a knobbly lump just like a nose and two dents for eyes. It had a smiling, wonky crack of a mouth.

"Hello," said Ruby. The rock didn't reply.

She picked the rock up. It was as heavy as the baby next door.

She put the rock up close to
her ear, but it was silent. She
whispered to it, but it didn't reply.

She breathed in its cold cellar
smell. Nothing like the kitten . . .
but it did smile. Ruby smiled
back.

"I've got a pet! I'VE GOT A
PET!" She rushed into the kitchen.
"LOOK!"

Ruby put the rock on the table. Jane and their parents came to look at Ruby's pet.

Jane laughed. "That's a stone."

Mum stroked it. "It's a very nice one," she said.

Dad turned it around in his hands and examined it carefully as if it were very precious. "It's a very fine specimen."

"Is it?" asked Ruby. "Oh, I've got a pet specimen. It must have fallen out of the sky."

Dad grinned. "From Planet Droppablock, perhaps?"

"Yes," said Ruby. "I think I'll call it Rocky. Rocky from Planet Droppablock. My pet."

"That's just so silly," said Jane. "It can't be from another planet. Anyway, there's no such thing as a pet rock. A pet has got to be alive. It's got to breathe!"

Ruby didn't say anything.
She stared at her smiling rock.
That was a tough one. It had
to breathe. Huh.

"Trees breathe," said Mum,
"you just can't see them doing it."

"Aha! See!" cried Ruby. "It *is*
alive!"

Chapter Three

Jane took Kitty to her room. She found a cardboard box and cut a doorway in it so Kitty could squeeze in and out. She put in an old jumper and an old cuddly monkey. Kitty went straight inside and rolled on her back and tussled with the monkey. When the monkey was dead she ran in and out chasing her tail.

Ruby watched, thinking, Huh! She found a shoe box still lined with tissue paper and put in a scrap of blanket. "This will make a lovely bed," she told her rock. She had lots of cuddly toys on her bed, but none she could spare.

"I hope you won't be lonely, Rocky," she said as she took the box down to the playroom.

Then she remembered the pebbles in her pocket. "These'll keep you company." She slipped the pebbles into the box – three smooth and two knobbly – and laid the rock on top.

"There," she whispered. "That's cosy, isn't it?"

Jane came in. Kitty was snuggled under her chin, purring. "What are you doing?" she asked.

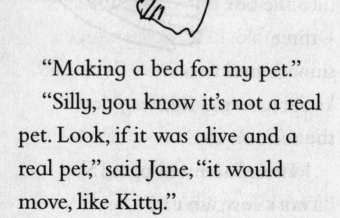

"Making a bed for my pet."
"Silly, you know it's not a real pet. Look, if it was alive and a real pet," said Jane, "it would move, like Kitty."

Ruby stroked her rock. It was
cold and hard and it didn't move.
"Things are different on Planet
Droppablock. It moves so, so, so
slowly, you can't see it," she said.
"Like a very, very, very slow
snail."

Jane's mouth fell open. She
didn't know what to say.

Ruby liked it when Jane was lost for words. She smiled. And the rock went on smiling too.

Jane sat down and Kitty leaped around the room, bouncing over the chairs and fluffing up her tail like a brush.

"Shame your pet is so slow," Jane said, throwing a sponge ball for Kitty. "I mean, you can't have much fun with such a slow pet, can you?"

"Huh," said Ruby.

Kitty jumped and cartwheeled around the room after the ball, leaping on invisible mice and chewing her cuddly monkey.

Then Ruby noticed something: the kitten had made a puddle on the floor.

"Mum! Mum!" she called.

"What is it?"

Ruby pointed. "That naughty Kitty's made a puddle," she said quietly.

"Oh dear, never mind," said Mum. "That's what kittens do. Jane must clear it up."

Jane made a face. "Yuck! It's smelly. I don't want to."

Ruby sat beside her rock and

stroked it. "I'm glad you don't do things like that, Rocky," she said. "What a good, well-trained pet you are."

Jane scowled.

That night, when Jane went up to bed, she took Kitty with her. The kitten curled up on the bed and purred and went to sleep.

Ruby put Rocky on her bed.
The rock was finding it hard to
settle down, so Ruby sang it a
lullaby.

"What's all that noise? Why
are you singing?" asked Jane,
peering into Ruby's room. "It's
not real," she added, eyeing the
rock on Ruby's bed. You know it's
not. You're just pretending."

Ruby smiled a big, secretive smile. She shrugged. "Goodnight, Jane, and shut the door please – I don't want Rocky to get out in the night."

"It's not alive, Ruby, it really isn't!" cried Jane. "Look, if you say it's not alive and not a real pet, you can give Kitty her breakfast in the morning."

"No thank you. And don't shout, you'll wake Rocky."

"Oh, you drive me mad!" Jane was just about to slam the door shut when she had a thought. "I suppose you'll be too busy to feed Kitty in the morning because you'll be feeding your stone, won't you?"

Ruby looked blank.

"No? Why not, Ruby? Why doesn't your stone eat anything? I'll tell you why. Because it's NOT ALIVE!"

And then she *did* slam the door.

Chapter Four

There was going to be a church
fête on Saturday. A leaflet came
through the door with all the
details of what was going to be
there.

"Look," said Jane. "There are lots of competitions for pets. I'm going to enter Kitty for the cuddliest kitten competition."

Ruby stared at her. "Huh," she said, "what about me?" She grabbed the sheet of paper from Jane.

"Silly. You haven't got a pet."

"I have. I'm going to enter my pet rock," said Ruby.

"You can't, it's not real."

"I can. It is. It'll win too."

"You can't! Mum, please don't let Ruby enter her stupid stone in the competition," cried Jane. "Everyone will laugh. Ruby, why are you so annoying?"

"I don't know," said Ruby. "Listen, if I *do* win, then you've got to let me share Kitty with you ..."

"No!" said Jane.

"Just a bit. Just let me play with her a bit. That would be fair ... if I win."

"Oh, OK ... but you won't win!"

"We shall see," said Ruby mysteriously.

Jane spent hours getting Kitty ready for the competition. She brushed her black fur until it gleamed and sprinkled her with perfume so she smelled like an exotic flower. When Kitty was quite ready, Jane tied a pink ribbon around her neck.

Ruby watched and when Jane had finished, Ruby got her rock

ready. First she cleaned Rocky
with soap. When
it was spotless,
she dried it.
Then she
rubbed it with
olive oil until it gleamed. Next,
she got a small box and painted
the inside blue and green with
silver squiggles. She filled the box
with moss and
leaves and rose
petals to make
a wonderful
nest for her
rock.

There was one small window
where you could look inside and
when you did peer through, it
was all murky and mysterious.
The rock sat amongst the petals

and leaves like a peculiar, very
still, smiling toad. Ruby made a
label for it:

*Rocky the Marvellus Misteeriyus
Rock Monsta from Planit Droppablok*

"No prizes for spelling," said
Jane. "You don't think it's going
to win the cuddliest kitten
competition, do you? It can't."

"We're not going to even try to
win the cuddliest kitten
competition," said Ruby. "I'm not
stupid."

44

There were all sorts of animals
in the competition. Children
brought cats, dogs, lizards, frogs,
stick insects, snakes and even a
caterpillar.

Jane and Ruby wandered
around looking at all the pets.

"Well? Where are you going to put your stone?" asked Jane. "It's a bit hard to find the right place for such a *fascinating* and *exciting* animal, isn't it?"

Ruby smiled in a superior way. "Don't worry," she said, carrying her box further

along past the fluffiest bunnies and the prettiest puppies.

"How about entering it in this category?" asked Jane, pointing at the label: BEST BEHAVED PET. "I mean, it is well behaved, isn't it?"

"No, I'm putting it here," said Ruby.

And she put the box on a table with the label: MOST UNUSUAL PET.

47

Lots of people came and stared at the mysterious Monster from Planet Droppablock. The rock sat very still and looked very unusual. When the judge looked in through the tiny window, she gasped in surprise. She put on her glasses and peered at it again and grinned. The rock smiled back.

It won first prize.

"It's a rare and fabulous beast," laughed the judge. "I've never seen such an unusual and well-behaved monster from such a faraway planet. Well done!"

When the judge had passed on to consider the next group of pets, Jane said, "That's not fair! You always get your way, Ruby. It's not fair!"

"Why?" asked Ruby.

"Well, it's not even a real pet. You shouldn't even have a pet until you're eight!"

"It is a pet if I cuddle it and keep it clean. I look after it and take it to bed with me.

It keeps me company and it is my best friend so then it *is* my pet."

"Ooooh!" Jane was so furious, she grabbed the Mysterious Monster from Planet Droppablock's box and pulled it open. She yanked out the rock and held it up.

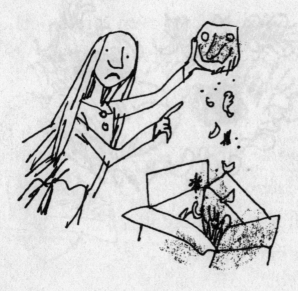

"Look, it's just a stone, it's not a monster at all – it isn't even alive—"

She stopped and stared into the nest. There were five pebbles nestling in the moss – three smooth and two knobbly.

"What are those?"

"Didn't I tell you it had
babies?" asked Ruby quietly. "I
must have forgotten."

Jane dropped the rock.
"Babies?"

"Oh, mind Rocky! Yes . . .
babies." Ruby popped her prize-
winning rock back in
the box and closed
the lid.

"Oh, it's just
not fair!" Jane
would have burst
into angry tears,
but she didn't
because the judge
was just about to look
at the kittens. "Oh, Ruby!" was
all she said.

Jane and Ruby crept up behind
the judge as she strolled

up and down beside the table,
peering at the kittens in the
cages.

"Kitty looks perfect!"
whispered Jane.

"I'm sure she'll win," Ruby whispered back. "She is the most cuddly kitten in the world," she added kindly.

When the judge picked Kitty up, the kitten scrambled up beneath the judge's chin and purred.

"The winner!" announced the
judge. "Definitely the cutest and
cuddliest kitten I've ever met!"

Chapter Five

When they got home, Jane and
Ruby took their pets into the
playroom. Both of them had
rosettes. Both were winners.

"I'm glad Kitty won," said Ruby.

"Thanks."

"You can look at my rock's babies if you want."

Jane stroked her rosette thoughtfully. "You can play with Kitty whenever you like, Ruby."

"Thanks," said Ruby.

Ruby placed her rock gently on the floor. "It's tired after the fête," she said.

"Ruby, you know it isn't . . ."
began Jane. But she stopped. The
kitten had suddenly noticed the
rock and was staring at it in
amazement. The stone face stared
back.

Kitty began to creep up on the
rock, stalking it, imagining it was
a dangerous creature.

Suddenly she
pounced, landing
right on top of
the rock, but her
claws couldn't hold
on and she slithered off,
rolling and
tumbling in a
furry ball. She
darted round
the rock and tried

again and again, slipping off
each time. Finally
she sank down
beside the rock
and licked it.

Jane giggled.

"They're going to be best friends," said Ruby.

"I hope so," said Jane.

Ruby smiled. She was so looking forward to playing with Kitty. She'd make toys for her

and cardboard tunnels to run
through and make Kitty like
her so much she would sleep on
her bed too. She knew how to
look after a pet, all right. She
grinned. It was going to be
such fun.

Rocky from Planet
Droppablock went on smiling
too.

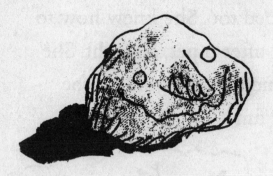

THE END